D1564808

ALICE IN VERSE
THE LOST RHYMES OF
WONDERLAND

ALICE IN VERSE
THE LOST RHYMES OF
WONDERLAND

J. T. HOLDEN

ILLUSTRATIONS BY

ANDREW JOHNSON

Candlestone
Books
for the
Imagination

Chicago   New York

All rights reserved.
Published by Candleshoe Books, in association with Flores-Deter
3122 N. California Avenue, Suite 3L Chicago, Illinois 60618
CANDLESHOE, the WAX SEAL LOGO, and associated logos are
trademarks and/or registered trademarks of Candleshoe Books.

CIP data available

Library of Congress Control Number: 2009931073

ISBN-13: 978-0-9825089-9-2 • ISBN-10: 0-982-50899-9

10 9 8 7 6 5 4 3 2 1

Printed in the U.S.A.
First Edition, December 2009

For

Kathy & Sherri

&

Jo

TABLE OF CONTENTS

List of Illustrations

INTRODUCTION

In 1865 Charles Lutwidge Dodgson published *Alice's Adventures in Wonderland* under the pen-name Lewis Carroll. The sequel, *Through the Looking-Glass & What Alice Found There*, followed in 1871. During the nine years Dodgson spent writing the two books that would cement his pen-name and reputation in children's literature for generations to come, he had compiled numerous poems and snippets of verse—only a scant number of which ultimately made their way onto the pages of his masterpiece and its sequel. Shortly after Dodgson's death at the age of 66 in 1898, rumours began to surface of 'the lost rhymes'—a collection of poetry that presumably shed more light on the subject of Wonderland and the Looking-Glass world. Understandably, questions abounded: Who *really* stole the Queen's tarts? Whatever *did* become of the Walrus and the Carpenter *after* their nefarious jot down the briny beach with the little Oysters? Is there truly *any* sense to be found in nonsense at all?

Of course, this was all highly speculative. No one had ever actually *seen* these so-called 'lost rhymes'—and if in fact they *had* existed in the first place, it was generally assumed the author had taken the secret of their whereabouts with him...

That is the tale, as told by my grandfather, back in a time when I was still small enough to settle on his knee for a story— long before I ever put pen to paper, or had the slightest notion that I would one day make a living telling stories. Now, in the spirit of full disclosure, it should be noted that my grandfather was both an Irishman and a storyteller (which, arguably, are one and the same) and had long been known to put a little polish on a story from time to time—that is, of course, when he wasn't making one up out of whole cloth. But whether or not the legend of the Lost Rhymes was merely a product of a clever old man's imagination, spun solely for the entertainment of an inquisitive boy with a depthless capacity for puzzles, mysteries, and all things unattainable, was inconsequential. The seed had been planted, and already experimental tendrils had begun poking up from the soil. If there was even a *grain* of truth to the tale, the *slightest* chance that the Lost Rhymes might possibly be out there, I was certain that I would find them. Or so I believed back in those heady days of the 'unclouded brow and dreaming eyes of wonder'.

Sometime during the inevitable transition from adolescence to adulthood, the dream of discovery was replaced by the discovery of a new, more tangible dream: I had begun to put words on paper. My own words. And even the long-standing lure of the elusive Lost Rhymes couldn't keep me from this wonderful new sensation of creating stories and rhymes of my own. As time passed, the Lost Rhymes receded further into the reaches of 'Memory's mystic band'. And yet the *idea* of them— the spark that lit the flame that fuels my creativity to this very day—remained, like a slow-burning ember, waiting for someone to stoke the kindling on the grate above it...

It was while working revisions on a book of spooky poems based upon legends, faerie tales, and folklore that a time-worn question popped into my mind, quite unexpectedly, and no matter how hard I tried to push it back and get on with the task at hand, it would not relent. It was a simple question, yet one that opened myriad doors down that long and dimly-lit corridor of my childhood: *Who* really *stole the Queen's tarts?* As I pondered this question (along with others—*Whatever* did *become of the Walrus and the Carpenter? Is there* any *sense to be found in nonsense?*), I found myself drifting further away from my spooky rhymes and closer to those long-sought Lost Rhymes of Wonderland. A thorough search of every library and internet site that contained any information on Carroll and his works produced nothing. Were the Lost Rhymes truly lost? Had they ever existed in the first place? Was I just wasting my time, hunting the ghost in the hall, as my grandfather used to say?

It was in this moment of thoughtful introspection—and, admittedly, doubt—that an exchange between my grandfather and me resurfaced. I couldn't have been more than seven at the time. I don't recall where we were, whether it was night or day, or whether indeed the exchange was simply the product of a dream, but, real or dreamt, the moment remains etched in my memory. I had asked him if he believed anyone would ever find the Lost Rhymes, and though his reply came with a wink, there was no sign of guile: 'If anyone is to find them, it will be you.'

As those words settled in, and doubt began to give way to clarity and conviction, I couldn't help feeling that somewhere my grandfather was smiling. With this vital clue in hand, and a renewed sense of faith in the fable, I set forth in search of the Lost Rhymes once again—only, this time, my journey began on a single blank page and ended with the book you now hold in your hands.

J. T. Holden
2009

Thus grew the tale of Wonderland:
Thus slowly, one by one,
Its quaint events were hammered out—
And now the tale is done...

— LEWIS CARROLL

Alice in Verse
The Lost Rhymes of
Wonderland

DOWN THE RABBIT-HOLE AGAIN

How doth the morning sunlight breach
  The shade beneath the thickets,
Along the bank, across the reach,
  To still the song of crickets.

How drowsily the blades of grass
  Sway on the subtle breezes,
Which waft about the bonny lass
  Who lounges as she pleases.

How languid is her study pose,
  How leisurely she strays
From 'neath the throes of dreary prose
  To more poetic days.

How longingly she recollects
  Those mem'ries most arousing—

The puzzling paths that intersect
    Her consciousness when drowsing.

How lovely spill her silky locks,
    How sweetly drops her jaw
When first she spies the clock of clocks
    Within the Rabbit's paw.

How swiftly to the wooded stop
    Beneath the sunny knoll:
How deep and dark her sudden drop
    Into the rabbit-hole…

The Bottle & the Biscuit Box

Along the narrow passageway,
  Beneath the dreamy glow
Of muted light from hanging lamps,
  All lined up in a row.
Into the hall of many doors,
  Upon the little table
A bottle sits, and round its neck:
  A *most* inviting label.

No hope to breach the smallest door—
  Perhaps then she should drink it.
And *yet* it could be *poisonous*—
  Perhaps she should *rethink* it.
A bottle labeled 'poison' is
  Most sure to disagree—
Contrariwise, from ill effects,
  One *surely* would be free!

How curious the flavour spills
    Along the dwindling throat!
How high the little table grows—
    How *terribly* remote.
The perfect drink to make one shrink,
    One surely would agree;
The perfect size for entry, true—
    But *not* without the *key*.

Beneath the soaring table now:
    A tiny biscuit box—
And there within, a little sin:
    A *tasty* paradox.
A little bite, perhaps it might
    Reverse—to some degree—
The ill-effect and redirect
    Up to the mocking key.

How curious the morsel slides
    Along the stretching throat!
How *scarcely* does the hall of doors
    Accommodate the *bloat*.
The perfect dough to make one grow,
    One surely can't deny.

And *yet* the key still out of reach—
    Enough to make one cry!

Another sip, another bite
    Could do but modest harm—
A little more to reach the floor
    Might prove to be the charm!
How doth the proper measurements
    Indeed erase all fears—
How swiftly one is swept away
    Upon a pool of tears!

The Caterpillar's Lesson on Rhetoric & Rhyme

Through the sun-dappled forest of towering grass,
Where a long trail of smoke leads the way to the pass
'Neath the shade of the flowers in full summer bloom,
Where the wisest of orators rests on his 'shroom—
With his mind ever-sharp, and his tongue ever-terse,
As he lectures on dialect, doggerel, and verse:

'Your poetry's *rough*—an affront to the ear
That is trained for the rhythm that we practice here.
It should travel with ease from your tongue to your mouth,
Like the winds from the north as they travel down south.

Like the moon in ascension, or stars on the breeze,
Should the verbal intention be *always* to please—
To traverse the vernacular we practice here,
To the rules of these rhythms, so *must* you adhere:

You should never include more than what is required
Of the verse you rehearse for results most desired—
For the troublesome stanza, you've probably heard,
Is the one that is burdened by *one* extra word.

Now these phrases poetic may often sound queer—
Rearranged, interchanged, and exceedingly drear—
But a word thus omitted is song to the ear
Of the *sweet* elocution that we practice here.

So always remember to keep tempo true,
And be mindful of diction—no matter the skew—
And to flip your words freely, but *never* exceed
All those requisite syllables that you will need.

We shall start with the basics of rhythm and rhyme,
And thus count every syllable whilst keeping time—
Without heed to the logic that others hold dear,
Or resistance to phrases you'd often find queer.

So, if thusly possessed, I suggest you regale
With the *frightful* delight of a *maritime* tale.
I shall cue you but once; then you're off on your own,
Yet to tease with your rhythm and please with your tone:

How Doth the Little Busy Bee
        Or *Crocodile* begin it—
Now give us song as twice as long,
        With more *compunction* in it.
But mindful of the syllables
        And tempo as you spin it—
For less or more, or cadence poor,
        Will surely *never* win it.'

The Mariner's Tale

With comportment in question and hands folded so,
She commenced with recital of maritime woe—
With a tone most peculiar, which only grew worse
With the trembling release of each subsequent verse:

> 'How doth the looming middle-night
>   Continue with its breathing—
> To overlay what underlies,
>   And propagate such seething!
>
> How skillfully they navigate,
>   How steadily they row
> About the sea in search of things
>   So many miles below.
>
> How deeply plunge the divers here
>   Into the blackest waters—

To slay the creature whilst she sleeps
  Beside her sons and daughters.

How boldly they perform their task,
  How silent then the wake,
As creatures small begin to stir,
  With hungers yet to slake.

How frenzied doth the waters flail
  To complement such seething—
How deafening *those foundlings wail,*
  When first they take to teething!'

THE SUBJECTIVE REVIEW

The Caterpillar closed his eyes,
　　And raised his pointed nose—
In cool contempt or careful thought,
　　Or simply in repose,
One couldn't say with certainty:
　　One *really* never knows.

He tapped his fingers pensively,
　　Whilst lavish rings of smoke
Did permeate about his perch
　　To form a shielding cloak—
And when the haze was quite replete,
　　The Caterpillar spoke:

'How lovely flows your melody,
　　How *sweet* your coarse refrain—
How perfectly you galvanise
　　The *perfectly* mundane.

15

How practical your poetry,
How timely every cue—
How clearly you infuse it with
A *clearly* slanted view.

How smooth your flow of syllables,
How *deft* your cutting wit—
How flawlessly you intertwine
Each *flawed* and tepid bit.

How sweetly blunt your countenance,
How picturesque your idyll—
However, you should *never* slouch
When offering recital!'

As silence fell about the wood,
The trees began to sway—
And when the smoke dispersed at last
(At much to her dismay)
The Caterpillar spread his wings,
And on them flew away.

The Cook, The Pig, The Cat & His Duchess

'Come straight to the kitchen; don't knock at the door,
    For the footman who sits on the stoop
Will be caught in the crossfire of dishes galore,
    As the fight rages over the soup!

Don't mind all the pepper, and please hold your sneezes—
    You'll only awaken the baby
That the Duchess is rocking, as *rough* as she pleases,
    Whilst dodging the boat and the gravy!

How she cradles her child with an unyielding mitt,
    As she muddles her way through the rhyme—
How she tosses it up and then violently shakes it
    To punctuate every last line!

Come hunker down here by the hearth where it's safe
    From the shower of saucepans and plates—

Come sit for a while near the cat with the smile,
    As the mayhem above culminates!

Now the Duchess and Cook are *indelibly* linked,
    Yet between them there's little remorse—
And suffice it to say that it's *only* by day
    They engage in such *heated* discourse.

At six the Cook leaves, and the poor Duchess grieves
 All those innocents recently weaned—
For the Cook serves by night a most *monstrous* delight
 At the court of the King and the Queen!

Now the Duchess, it's true, often dines at the court,
 Though she *seldom* consumes half her weight—
For well-plied with the port, she can still hear the snort
 Of the child she has cradled of late.

But it's not all as gruesome as one might opine—
 For the crux is quite simple indeed:
Though it's *true* the meat's royal upon which they dine,
 None are *Royals* upon which they feed!

Though the meat is quite tasty and goes well with wine
 (And with afters of treacle and figs)
I assure you the "children" upon which they dine
 Are but *only* the King's royal pigs!

'Tis the Cook's wicked wit, and the consequent fit
 Of the Duchess, that drives this old story—
'Tis a conflict of old that has seldom been told
 Of the fate of their shared porcine quarry!'

As the cat stretched his paws to reveal his fine claws,
    So the rest of him started to fade—
And what little remained was the grin that he feigned,
    As he spoke of the beast in the wabe.

'For directions,' he said, 'do be careful to tread
    Far away from the wabe in the wood:
You will find it more pleasant right here in the present—
    If not, then you probably should!

If you really must go, then it's best you should know
    That to *find* you need only to *seek*—
But in seeking and finding, you may need reminding:
    Once found, is what's sought worth a peek?

For *this* way, the Hatter: for *that* way, the Hare—
    Both are mad and exceedingly queer!
More likely than not you will find them together—
    Now, excuse me, whilst I disappear...'

The Tea Party Resumes

'No room!' cried the Hatter. 'No Room!' cried the Hare.
'Please join us at once! There is *no* room to spare!'
With the Mouse resting soundly, they offered a chair,
And at once, rather roundly, did Hatter declare:

'If to say what you mean is to mean what you say,
    Then to mean what you say, just repeat it—
Though you might just as well say *I see what I eat*
    Is the same as *I see thus I eat it!*'

'Or,' the Hare added smartly, *'I get what I like*
    Is the same as *I like what I'm getting!*
Or to *breathe when you sleep* is to *sleep when you breathe!*
    Or to *set something up* is *upsetting!*'

In his slumber, the Dormouse concurred with them both—
    Though, in truth, he was most likely dreaming

Of a tray filled with tarts and a deck full of Hearts
    Taking flight at Her Majesty's screaming.

'Clean cup!' cried the Hatter. 'Clean cup!' cried the Hare.
'Clean cups all around now! We've *no* cups to spare!'
With the mouse on the doily, they shifted their chairs,
And at once, rather coyly, did Hatter declare:

'If a story is sad at the end, is it bad
    To conclude with a happy beginning?
If apart from the start, it will tug at the heart,
    Should one start at the part that's most winning?'

'Or,' the Hare interjected, 'conclude at the part
 Where the tea is most *gleefully* flowing?
Could a story as such ever mean *quite* as much
 As another not *nearly* worth knowing?'

In his slumber, the Dormouse began to recite:
 'You must steal them all—every last one!
We shall divvy them fairly and savour each bite!
 To the garden now! Off with you! Run!'

'Such tales!' cried the Hatter. 'Such *lies!*' cried the Hare.
'Such stories as such one should *be* loathe to share!'
With the mouse still reciting, so did they repair
To seats more inviting, and left the mouse there.

'If the truth's in the telling,' said Hatter, 'beware—
 For the telling of truth's overrated!
And no matter the lies, 'tis a far better guise
 For the one who appears *less* than sated!'

'It is true,' the Hare added, 'but lest we forget:
 One should *always* create a diversion—
And the one so inclined to the taste *less* refined
 Is so *easily* led to subversion!'

In his slumber the Dormouse concurred once again,
    But before he could take up recital—
They plied him with tea, and a thick wedge of brie,
    Which sufficed just as nice as a bridle.

'More tea!' cried the Hatter. 'More tea!' cried the Hare.
'More tea, though you've had *less* than *more* of your share!'
With his eyes shining brightly, his posture foursquare,
And his lips curling spritely, did Hatter declare:

'We'll begin at the end and conclude at the start,
    For the start is the best place to end it,
Like the filling you suck with a straw from a tart—
    If you haven't, we *do* recommend it!'

'For a tart not to start with the *fine* treacle paste
    Is a waste of the space that's inside it:
For the tart that is chaste is a *terrible* waste—
    And one never knows *how* to divide it!'

'Here here!' cried the Hatter. 'There there!' cried the Hare.
'We've arrived at the end now! We've *no* time to spare!'
With the mouse in the teapot—and one empty chair—
Came the final recital of Hatter and Hare:

be   done

not   until

can-   it is

it   per-

'Now   fect,

Nor

perfect

until it

is done—

Whether

perfectly

done, or

yet done

to per-

fec-

tion,

when

done

per-

fect,

shall
it be
done!'

A Slight Detour Through the Looking-Glass

Through the deep tulgey wood, past the long-standing wabe,
    Where the Bandersnatch bellows and preys;
From the egg on the wall—and his subsequent fall—
    To a messenger's poignant malaise.

From a King's sheer delight at his Queen's rapid flight
    (And a bread that's *suspiciously* brown)
To a bold Crimson Knight and his counterpart White,
    And a battle of beasts for the crown.

At the top of the hill, past the garden of buds,
    Where the flowers recite, one and all—
Cross the checkerboard field, with its squares red and white,
    To the checkerboard floor of the hall.

Now come to the feast where the mutton's not least
    To be sliced or be served of the three—

With a pudding so chatty, and fish rather natty,
    Be welcomed here thirty times three!

With cats in the coffee and mice in the tea,
    With buttons and bran in the wine—
With the treacle and ink that is pleasant to drink,
    So be welcomed here ninety times nine!

DEE & DUM

'Shall we tell you a tale that you've not heard before?
If you have, then please stop us—if not, cry for more!
But if *less* you require from the coffers of yore,
Then perhaps you should travel to some other shore!

But don't run—not just yet—for you cannot ignore
That you haven't a clue what the wood holds in store:
All those dark little nooks that you bypassed before
Still await your impending and final encore!

It's safer back here from the things that you fear!
Like the raven, the rook—or the crow, if you please,
With his dark feathered wings that expand with such ease;
With his talons so sharp and his brilliant black beak
In contrariwise pose with the sound of his shriek.
From those things that you fear, it is *much* safer here!

Now we've settled the battle, and evened the score,
And divided the rattle in parts numb'ring four.
If you like, we can whittle them down furthermore:
Ten shillings, six pence—but not one penny more!

So the tale we regale with shall be evermore
But a fable of vengeance that *some* may deplore,
Whilst others, most wicked of heart, may adore:
The return of the two who once dined on the shore...'

The Walrus & the Carpenter
Head Back

The moon was shining on the sea,
    So to eclipse the sun:
She did her very best to make
    The billows roughly run—
And this was odd, because, of course,
    The day had just begun.

The sun was sulking in the gloom
    That swallowed up his light,
And set the skies he'd painted blue
    In shades of blackest night—
'It's very rude of her,' he cried,
    'To do this out of *spite*!'

The sands were dry as dry could be,
    The sea was wet as wet.

The air was foul and dank and thick
    With bittersweet regret—
The sort that weighs the heavy heart,
    And labours to forget.

The Walrus and the Carpenter
    Were heading back the way
They'd come from but an hour past,
    When night was plainly day—
Before the clouds had settled in,
    And filled the skies with grey.

'I did not think it quite so dark
    When first we headed out!
Do you suppose,' the Walrus said,
    'They've rearranged this route?'
'No question,' said the Carpenter,
    His heart yet filled with doubt.

'O come, my friend, let's rest a while,'
    The Walrus did implore.
'A little break to still the wake
    Along this briny shore:

We *cannot* take another step
    Beyond another four!'

The weary Builder gave a sigh,
    But not a word he said:
Into the dark he trudged along,
    Determined now for bed—
His belly thick with peppered swag,
    And vinegar and bread.

But slower still their footsteps fell
    Into the sinking sand,
Which rose—and swiftly—to their knees
    In striking countermand—
Whilst from the frothy breaking waves
    They came now, hand-in-hand.

Four dozen Oysters followed fast,
    And yet four *hundred* more;
And thick and quick, their bodies slick,
    They gathered on the shore—
All circling round and closing in,
    More eager than before.

'Dear Oysters, come and rally round!'
 The Walrus did beseech.
'It seems we've dipped into a rut
 Along this brackish beach:
It would be grand to lend hand—
 If four would give to each.'

The eldest Oyster gazed at him,
 And raised a clever brow.

The eldest Oyster nodded then,
    For this he did allow:
To lend a hand, it *would* be grand—
    But which to whom and how?

'A coil of thread,' the eldest said,
    'Is what we do require
To hoist them up and drag them out
    From 'neath this boggy mire—
Some kindling, too, and flint as well,
    To build a *warming* fire.'

'But not too hot!' the Walrus cried,
    As flames licked at his feet—
And yet the pyre burned high and bright,
    And ever-so replete—
Whilst wafting scents into the night
    Of *sweetest* sizzling meat.

'The time has come,' the Oysters cried,
    'To settle down to tea—
To break the bread and thickly spread
    The lard with zesty brie!'

'A little spice, that *would* be nice,'
    The eldest did agree.

'It was so very kind of you
    To grace us with this feast!'
But no reply the Walrus gave,
    Which scorned them not the least—
For full his maw and thick his craw
    With vinegar and yeast.

'It's seems a shame,' the Builder sobbed,
    'To bring this feast to shut.'
To which the eldest did agree,
    And none there could rebut—
And so they stoked the waning fire
    To satisfy their *glut*.

'O Carpenter, we weep for you!
    Dear Walrus, we lament
The boiling sea—and cabbages—
    Those kings of malcontent—
The shoes—and ships—and sealing-wax—
    And *all* that they ferment.'

'A pleasant run, you both have had—
    The *sights* that you have seen!
But now we must be trotting home,'
    They sighed, with sated mien—

And this was scarcely odd, because
    They'd licked their plates *quite* clean.

THE BATTLE

'Now we're done with our tale, and we *must* have a fight:
    We don't care if it lasts very long!
And though each of us feels *inexorably* right,
    We're not *certain* the other is wrong!'

'Now I've got a headache—it's *terribly* grim—
    But the battle cannot be postponed!'
'And *I've* got a toothache—I'm *far* worse than him—
    But a rematch cannot be condoned!'

'We shall fight until six, and then dine until dawn,
    And then sleep until midday or one!
Then we'll take up the battle—if but for the rattle—
    And cut down the trees, every one!'

'Now I generally hit everything I can see—
    Or at least what I see when excited!'

'And *I* hit all things within reach of my sword—
    Whether seeing or as yet unsighted!'

'Let the battle commence! Raise your sword, if you've one—
    And, if not, simply raise your umbrella!
But we *must* begin quickly! The sky's growing dark!
    And by night we recite *a cappella!*'

'Are you leaving so soon? We have yet to begin!
    If you go now, you'll miss all the action!
If you must, then be off to the court of the Queen—
    There you'll find a most *pleasant* distraction!'

'They have games in the garden, and tarts served with tea—
    Though their manners are often quite coarse!'
'They have trials, tribulations, and all sorts of glee—
    Though they seldom show any remorse!'

'So join them at once on the rose garden green,
    But be mindful of what we have said—
For the game that you win is a loss to the Queen,
    And a loss thus will cost you your head!'

In the Garden of Hearts

Now come to the place at the edge of the wood,
    Where the roses are lovely—yet *white*—
Where the Five and the Two and the Seven of Spades
    Have been frantically painting all night.

Come take your flamingo and hammer the hog
    Through the wickets of cards on the green—
But be mindful to send it straight into the bog
    Lest you challenge the wrath of the Queen!

Now look to the skies where the Cat's clever eyes
    Doth alight to the fright of the ring—
And the utter disdain of the monarchs who reign:
    That a cat may *dare* look at a King!

Come walk with the Duchess: she's done with her fit,
    And her manner is oddly serene;

She will give you the moral to every last wit
    That has ever endeavored or been.

Now follow the Gryphon, and hear the sad tale
    Of the Mock Turtle's school in the sea—
Where the Lobster Quadrille, if you won't or you will,
    Is the thrill of the court's coterie!

Come play for the day, but don't stay through the night,
    For the light in the night is quite thin.
Now onto the site where the sun's shining bright,
    And the trial is about to begin!

The Trial Begins

The King proclaimed the trial to start
    Upon the stroke of one clock,
And so, in turn, did rap his gavel
    On the varnished sound block.
'We first shall hear the evidence—
    And then commence the hanging!'
To quell ensuing cheers and jeers,
    His gavel took to banging.

As silence fell, the King deferred
    To counsel for the hoodlum;
And once again there rose a din
    That soon broke out in bedlam.
The gavel fell to crush the swell,
    And bring the court to order.
With regal voice, the charge was read
    At once by the reporter:

'The Queen of Hearts, she made some tarts,
     All on a summer day:
The Knave of Hearts, he stole those tarts,
     And took them quite away!
The Knave of Hearts returned the tarts
     Still later that same day;
And with them came his earnest shame,
     And all was right and gay!'

The Hatter, seated near the Knave,
    As counsel most beguiling,
Exchanged a snort about this tort
    With counsel counter-filing.
The Hare then shook his tawny head,
    Whilst winking unassuming,
And strode up to the witness box,
    With posture most presuming.

'The facts are clear as evidenced:
    The tarts were *clearly* taken—
And then returned, without a bite:
    On this, be not mistaken!
It's true a crime here has been done,
    But *whom* here is the victim—
With tasty treats returned un-ate,
    As if he'd never nicked them?'

He paused to let this settle in,
Before applying final spin:

'This trial is but a mockery
    Of justice and contrition—

57

If served with *tarts* but not with *tea*
To supplement nutrition!
If such it be—this travesty—
This humble court's position,
Then you, and me, and he, and she
Be guilty of sedition!'

At this, the King of Hearts concurred—
    To rounds of boisterous cheering—
And so he brought the gavel down
    At once to halt the hearing.
As tea was poured and tarts were passed
    Around the courtroom freely,
Both Hare and Hatter raised their cups,
    And sipped away genteelly.

When cups were drained and plates were cleaned
    Of tea and tarts delicious—
When all consumed, the court resumed
    With matters most judicious:
'We've heard the charge brought by the Hare
    Upon this crucial matter.
And now, before we hang this rogue,
    We'll listen to the Hatter…'

THE HATTER'S DEFENCE

'Now the devil you know is the better on par
    Than the devil you don't, strictly speaking—
For the devil you don't is more devilish by far
    Than the devil whose sins you're critiquing!

He's a thief and a liar—of this we are sure—
    But he's also quite handsome and strapping;
And although he'll conspire, his motives are pure—
    And he looks like an *angel* whilst napping!

He's a troublesome lad—though his manners aren't bad—
    And it's true that he stole from the Queen;
But his story's complex and *remarkably* sad—
    And his *form* is quite lovely and lean!

He's a mischievous rogue, with the mien of a prince,
    And the mane of a god—only *neater*—

With the sweetest of smiles and the deepest of dints—
    And the *rest* of him looks even *sweeter!*

He is carefully groomed and *suspiciously* clean,
    With a hygiene beyond expectation:
You'd be hard-pressed to find a more *un*soiled teen
    Who is riper for decapitation!

He's a rascal, a bounder, a basher, a boy,
    And it's true that he's often confounding—
Yet he's patently charming and blatantly coy,
    And the ladies all find him *astounding!*

He has dark, dreamy eyes, and a lovely pale throat—
    Though, in truth, it is ripe for the stretching!
He will pillage your pies and then openly gloat—
    Still, the devil you know is *quite* fetching!

So bring on your verdict, your blade and your rope,
    And we'll rally his swift execution—
If so *chilled* is your heart to the wiles of this mope,
    And the *swell* of this *grand* elocution!'

The Hare's Rebuttal
& the Hatter's Rebuke

With the evidence laid, so the jury was bade
    To retire for a judicious huddle—
'Neath the cover of shade at the rose colonnade,
    There to sort out this dubious muddle—
But their premature run was cut short half-past-one
    By the verse of the March Hare's rebuttal:

    'The Queen of Hearts, she made some tarts
        Upon a summer's morning:
    The Knave of Hearts, he came along,
        And *stole* them without warning!
    There's little more or less to say—
        Unless he pleads *suborning*;
    If not, then round his lovely neck
        A noose shall be adorning!
    I'm sure my colleague would agree,'
    The Hare concluded cheekily.

The Hatter merely sipped his tea,
Then smashed the cup quite suddenly.
'And *if*, by *that*, you do imply
    This *brute* that I'm defending
Was so *inclined* to thievery
    Upon *another's* wending,
You may do well to *reassess*
    The *message* that you're sending—
For *three* can swing as well as *one*,
    With verdicts yet *impending!*'

At this, the Hare demurred at length,
  Until the point was sinking—
To depths untravelled, deep within,
  Where warning signs were blinking.
'I pray the court forgive my most
  Erroneous rebuttal—
I hence defer to my consort
  Whose mind is less a muddle.
The act of this malicious brute
Was his *alone*, without dispute!'

With rebut laid to rest by rebuke sharply stressed,
  And the gavel at once interceding—
With the loopholes addressed, and the jurors abreast
  Of all evidence, fair and misleading—
With the sun in the west, at the good King's behest,
  There was time for yet one final pleading…

THE KNAVE OF HEARTS REPENTS

The Knave was gathered to the fore,
    Still shackled, wrist and ankle,
And forced upon the witness floor,
    As feathers took to rankle—
The jurors being mostly fowl
Would often flap their wings and yowl.

The Knave stood tall and handsomely
    Upon the witness planking,
And waited, rather patiently,
    Until they'd quelled their cranking—
A careful lad, and most polite,
So *carefully* he did recite:

'*How doth the shade of midnight bleed*
    The moonlight that it teases,
Yet stanch the flow of every ray
    That ultimately pleases.

How casually it mitigates
All feelings of compunction;
How thoroughly it permeates
At each and every junction.

How darkly spreads its chilly grasp
About the night to seize us,
And whispers through the highest boughs
With scornful *little breezes.*

How swiftly does it still the flows
Along the running rivers,
And wilt the budding garden rose
That tenuously quivers.

How gently doth the ruling hand
Embrace the lovely flower,
And so insure its swift remand
Into her ivory tower.

How doth she prize the sweet perfume,
With mercy most judicious,
When there it blooms, within her rooms,
To serve her as she wishes!'

A silence fell about the court,
    And echoed round the garden,
As none there offered up retort
    To circumvent the pardon—
None there at all, except the King,
Whose regal voice at once did ring:

'A touching verse!' the King declared.
    'A moving recitation!
But should the lad be thusly spared,
    And offered vindication?
I cannot rule, for all I've seen—
And so it falls unto the Queen…'

THE QUEEN'S SENTENCE

The Queen released a heaving sigh
    That shook the palace gables,
And sent a wave of turbulence
    Along the garden tables—
As tears began to freely flow,
    And flood the nearby stables.
And when the flow was stanched at last,
So did the Queen embrace her task:

'I made a tray of treacle tarts
    (We know this to be true)
And garnished each with tiny hearts
    Of lovely crimson hue.

I gave him one, he gave them three,
    They gave each other four;
Then all returned from him to me
    (Still two shy of a score).

They told me he had been to *her*,
    And mentioned me to *them*,
Who'd sullied my good character,
    And painted me so *grim*.

If *they* or *she* should chance to be
    Involved in this affair,
Then trust that we shall hang *all three*
    With swift judicious care!'

The Queen fell into silence, whilst
    The Hatter and the Hare
Did contemplate such violence with
    A most indifferent air—
And sipped their tea quite casually,
    As if they'd not a care.
They waited with sedated mien
To hear the ruling of the Queen:

'It's true, the crime committed here
    By *three* may have been done—
And yet the *theft*, it would *appear*,
    Was carried out by *one*.

Yet one of whom, one *must* admit,
　　Beyond one's modest measure,
It could be said one *might* acquit—
　　If *so* one's royal pleasure.

A notion that one *could* explore,
　　With little trepidation,
If *not* for one who would ignore
　　Such *tender* supplication.

Still torn my soul and pained my heart
　　Upon this weighty matter:
To spare the thief who stole the tarts,
　　Or send him up the ladder?'

The Queen approached the fated Knave,
　　Who knelt upon one knee,
Yet held his head up, high and brave,
　　For all the court to see—
A *handsome* head, it had been said,
　　And *none* could disagree.
As tears began to flow once more,
So did her final verse outpour:

'How gently flows the poetry,
    How smooth the sweet refrain;
How deeply cuts the lovely rose
    Into the regal vein.

How yet this dark and lonely night
    About us tempts and teases;
How, too, this ever-waning light
    So thoroughly displeases.

How carefully the ruling hand
    Doth cut the budding flower,
And thus ensure its safe remand
    Into the royal tower.

How deeply shall it please the host
    To view the lovely head—
Atop the highest corner post
    Above the royal bed!'

THE ROYAL FLUSH

The King reviewed the evidence,
    The Mouse began to scurry,
The Hatter brought the hammer down,
    The Hare prepared the curry.
They trapped the Mouse; the King cried out
    (As if there'd been no flurry):
'We'll carry out the sentence first,
    And then hear from the jury!'

The court concurred most heartily,
    And promptly took to cheering.
The Knave approached the chopping block,
    His final moment nearing.
Whilst Hare and Hatter plied the Mouse
    With soothing elocution,
There rose a voice in bold dissent
    To halt the execution:

'You cannot have the sentence first!
　　That's not the way it's doing!'
'You mean it's *done*,' the Hatter said,
　　'*Unless* I'm misconstruing—
If not, my dear, then hold your tongue,
　　Until the tea is brewing!'
'Or, if you *must*,' the Hare put in,
　　'At *least* until it's spewing!'

The Dormouse squeaked, the Hatter shrieked,
    The Hare was off and running—
Though twice as quick, not *near* as slick,
    Nor nearly *quite* as cunning!
The Mouse ran up the balustrade,
    The Hatter blocked the railing,
The King released the royal guard,
    The jury took to flailing.

'Collar that Mouse and turn him out!'
    The Queen of Hearts was screaming.
'Off with his whiskers! Off with his head!'
    (*'Wake up, dear Alice, you're dreaming!'*)
'Suppress him and pinch him and pepper his tail!
    And butter him up till he's gleaming!
Then bring me his head in a treacle-filled pail!'
    (*'Dear Alice, wake up now, you're dreaming!'*)

WAKING

She wakes with a start at the most frightful part:
    With a flurry of cards still descending;
With the Hare and the Hatter, the King and the Queen,
    And all others now swiftly ascending—

To the spot on the green where the Knave had once been,
    With the verdict of birds yet impending—
To the soft garden bed where the roses, now red,
    Are still wet with the freshness of mending—

To the trail of the twins, with their mischievous grins,
    And the rattle o'er which they're contending—
To the deep tulgey wood, past the long-standing wabe,
    Where the darkness is ever-descending—

To the party of tea, and the disgruntled three,
    And the cat with his smile condescending—

To the sage on his 'shroom, and the door-laden room,
  With a bottle and biscuit portending—

To that place in her dreams where the memory seems
  More and more like a happier ending—
To that moment in time where both rhythm and rhyme
  Are but virtues still *well worth defending*.

Alice! a childish story take,
And with a gentle hand
Lay it where Childhood's dreams are twined
In Memory's mystic band...

About the Author:

J. T. Holden is the author of the forthcoming books *Bedtime Tales for Naughty Children* and *O The Dark Things You'll See!* As a boy J. T. would often make up rhymes and limericks to entertain friends, but it wasn't until one of them gave him a gift-wrapped box containing a blank notebook and a pen that he took that first crucial step.

About the Illustrator:

Andrew Johnson currently works artistic venues in the Chicago area. An aficionado of all-things-Wonderland, it was Andrew's childhood dream that he would one day create illustrations for an *Alice in Wonderland* book.

ACKNOWLEDGEMENTS

J. T. Holden would like to thank

Lori A. Woolf
for that dark and spooky autumn night;
for that unmistakable laugh;
for making me believe I could
write a poem in the first place.

Beverly Brock
for that moment in a darkened theatre;
for teaching me how to drive a
5-speed manual transmission;
for that certain summer.

&

Jan Jeanblanc
for guiding me through the botanic gardens,
beyond whose gates what memories
continue to feed my creative soul;
for all those late-night chats by the warm glow
of the pumpkin lantern in the kitchen window;
for taking in an orphan and caring for him as your own:
no natural son was ever more loved,
and I am proud to call you my mother.

SPECIAL THANKS TO

Jean Kunold
Laura Forney
Lynne Kuefler
Kris Stevens
at
WorldColor Press

Julia Maguire
at
Simon & Schuster

Eric Platou
at
Malloy Incorporated

Karen Douglas
John Amabile
at
Vintage Graphic Arts LTD.

&

Paul Fiorelli
at
FiorelliGraphics & Printing

for their invaluable assistance.

This book was edited by J. Sparrow and
art directed by Michael John Puckett. The
text was set in Adobe Garamond Pro. The display
type was set in Occidental. The art for the cover was
drawn in Adobe Photoshop. The art for the interiors
was created using graphite on paper. The book
was printed at WorldColor Press Fairfield
(formerly: Quebecor World Fairfield)
in Fairfield, Pennsylvania. The
cover was printed at Vintage
Graphic Arts LTD in
Plainview, New
York.